Ruth Miskin's

Superphonics

Turquoise Storybook

The Story
of Dragonclaw

by Gill Munton

Illustrated by Beccy Blake

Hodder
Children's
Books

a division of Hodder Headline Limited

In the frozen north, there's a windswept place

Where the days dawn chilly and raw,

Where, long ago, two men gave chase

To a monster called Dragonclaw.

The story begins with the King of that land

As he stands at the castle door,

And vows he will give his daughter's hand

To the man who tames Dragonclaw!

And here's Lord Thumpjaw, greedy and bold

Uncorking some wine on his lawn,

And dreaming of Princess Gloria's gold,

As he gives a lazy yawn.

"On Snort, my horse,

and with Squawk on my arm

I'll gallop to Dragonclaw's cave ..."

But Squawk the hawk hears this with alarm:

"He treats me like a slave!

He gives me dirty water to drink,

And that stale corn is not very nice!

And if I want to take forty winks –

He sends me off to catch mice!

It's 'Your Lordship this',

and 'Your Lordship that',

It's enough to make a hawk spit!

If I get the chance, I will knock him flat –

I've had enough of it!"

And this is Rory, poor Rory, the groom,

Asleep on the stable floor,

Dreaming of Gloria at her loom

As he snores on his bed of straw.

He's loved the girl with the cornflower eyes

From the day that she was born.

"And now my chance has come!" he cries

As he wakes on this chilly grey morn.

"I have no horse, nor a hawk on my arm,

But I'll crawl on my hands and knees

For I've sworn on my sword,

   I will win you, ma'am,

I'll tame Dragonclaw with ease!"

In the morning, the men set out

For Dragonclaw's dark, dark cave,

First, Rory, with a joyful shout,

And then Thumpjaw, that greedy knave.

The two of them had plotted and planned

To return with Dragonclaw's skin.

The two of them wanted sweet Gloria's hand –

But only one could win.

Rory came to a frozen stream

Where the ice lay thick and black

He stepped upon it, in a dream ...

Rory, you must look back!

Squawk, warn him that Thumpjaw's

right behind!

But Squawk couldn't sing a note!

"This really is a very bad time

For a hawk to get a sore throat!"

Lord Thumpjaw laughed.

"I'm going to win!

Let's have a little sport!"

He cracked the ice – poor Rory fell in –

"That's the best place for your sort!"

Rory crawled out of the frozen stream,

With the help of his new pal, the hawk.

"You and me – we make a good team!"

Said the helpful hawk, with a squawk.

Next, he came to a screen of thorns.

But someone had got there first!

And someone looked at him with scorn ...

He's going to do his worst!

Squawk, warn him that Thumpjaw's

right behind!

But Squawk was sprawled on the floor.

"This really is a very bad time

For a hawk to get a sore claw!"

Lord Thumpjaw smiled, and cleared his throat.

He pushed Rory into the thorns.

"I've hurt my hand, and I've torn my coat!"

Lord Thumpjaw only yawned.

Rory crawled slowly out of the thorns.

The hawk limped at his side.

"Well, I think our brains will beat his brawn!

Come on, you run, and I'll fly!"

Next, they came to a mountain slope.

"There he is! The greedy lump!

He hasn't seen us yet, I hope,

And I know how to make Snort jump!"

Said Squawk, as he crawled down

  a narrow gap

In the rock, to the horse's tail.

"Squawk! Squawk! Let's go!

  Giddy-up, old chap!

Don't be such a snail!"

Snort sniffed the air, and flicked his ears,

And kicked his heels up high.

Lord Thumpjaw saw the ground draw near

And gave an awful cry.

They saw him roll down the mountainside.

They saw him roll into the hedge.

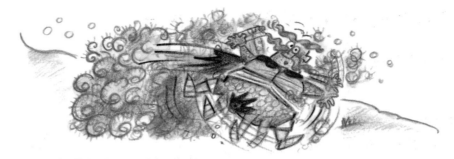

To the hole in the ice they saw him glide ...

And disappear over the edge!

"And now," said Rory, "for Dragonclaw!"

As he came to the monster's lair,

And Rory struck him on the jaw –

But Dragonclaw just STOOD there!

I know I'm a pest. I know I'm a pain.
But I'll never bother the King again.
I'll never darken the royal door –
If you'll call your first-born ...
Dragonclaw!

Rory went and told the King

Who did as he had sworn,

And Rory gave Gloria a wedding ring ...

And then Dragonclaw 2 was born!